THE CHAIN OF
DESTINY

BY

BRAM STOKER

British Library Cataloguing-in-Publication Data
A catalogue record for this book is available from the
British Library

CONTENTS

BRAM STOKER

Abraham 'Bram' Stoker was born in Dublin, Ireland in 1847. Stoker was a semi-invalid as a child, and was bedridden until he started school at the age of seven. However, he made a full recovery and went on to excel as an athlete at Trinity College, which he enrolled at in 1864. Stoker graduated with honours in mathematics in 1870, and was also president of the university's philosophical society.

Stoker developed an interest in theatre, and became theatre critic for the *Dublin Evening Mail* in his early twenties. It was following a favourable review he gave of an 1876 Henry Irving production of *Hamlet* that Stoker and Irving struck up a friendship. Three years later, in the same year that Stoker married Florence Balcombe (whose former suitor was Oscar Wilde), he became acting-manager and then business manager of Irving's Lyceum Theatre–a post he went on to hold for 27 years. As a result of his close friendship with Irving (the most famous actor of his day), Stoker became something of a socialite. He mingled with London's high society, meeting writers such as Sir Arthur Conan Doyle, and travelled extensively in the United States, where he spent time with both Theodore Roosevelt and Walt Whitman.

While working for Irving, Stoker began to write novels,

eventually producing a total of fifteen works of fiction. Although most met with at least mild success, Stoker is best known for his 1897 publication, *Dracula*. This work–an epistolary novel weaving hypnotism, magic, the supernatural, and other elements of Gothic fiction–went on to sell over one million copies, and has never been out of print. Today, the novel and its eponymous protagonist remain so well-known that one can actually visit the castle of Count Dracula in the Transylvanian region of Romania–despite the fact that Stoker never even went there himself.

After a series of strokes, Stoker died in London in 1912, aged 64.

THE CHAIN OF DESTINY

BRAM STOKER

1

A WARNING

It was so late in the evening when I arrived at Scarp that I had but little opportunity of observing the external appearance of the house; but, as far as I could judge in the dim twilight, it was a very stately edifice of seemingly great age, built of white stone. When I passed the porch, however, I could observe its internal beauties much more closely, for a large wood fire burned in the hall and all the rooms and passages were lighted. The hall was almost baronial in its size, and opened on to a staircase of dark oak so wide and so generous in its slope that a carriage might almost have been driven up it. The rooms were large and lofty, with their walls, like those of the staircase, panelled with oak black from age. This sombre material would have made the house intensely gloomy but for the enormous width and height of both rooms and passages. As it was, the effect was a homely combination of size and warmth. The windows were set in deep embrasures, and, on the ground story, reached from quite level with the floor to almost the ceiling. The fireplaces were quite in the old style, large and surrounded with massive oak carvings, representing on each some scene from biblical history, and at the side of each fireplace rose a pair of massive carved iron firedogs. It was altogether just such a house as would have delighted the heart of Washington Irving or Nathaniel Hawthorne.

The house had been lately restored; but in effecting the restoration comfort had not been forgotten, and any modern improvement which tended to increase the homelike appearance of the rooms had been added. The old diamond-paned casements, which had remained probably from the Elizabethan age, had given place to more useful plate glass; and, in like manner, many other changes had taken place. But so judiciously had every change been effected that nothing of the new clashed with the old, but the harmony of all the parts seemed complete.

I thought it no wonder that Mrs Trevor had fallen in love with Scarp the first time she had seen it. Mrs Trevor's liking the place was tantamount to her husband's buying it, for he was so wealthy that he could get almost anything money could purchase. He was himself a man of good taste, but still he felt his inferiority to his wife in this respect so much that he never dreamt of differing in opinion from her on any matter of choice or judgement. Mrs Trevor had, without exception, the best taste of any one whom I ever knew, and, strange to say, her taste was not confined to any branch of art. She did not write, or paint, or sing; but still her judgement in writing, painting, or music, was unquestioned by her friends. It seemed as if nature had denied to her the power of execution in any separate branch of art, in order to make her perfect in her appreciation of what was beautiful and true in all. She was perfect in the art of harmonising the art of everyday life. Her husband used to say, with a far-fetched joke, that her star must have been in the House of Libra, because everything which she said and did showed such a nicety of balance.

Mr and Mrs Trevor were the most model couple I ever knew–they really seemed not twain, but one. They appeared to have adopted something of the French idea of man and wife–that they should not be the less like friends because they were linked together by indissoluble bonds–that they should share their pleasures as well as their sorrows. The former outbalanced the latter, for both husband and wife were of that happy temperament which can take pleasure from everything, and find consolation even in the chastening rod of affliction.

Still, through their web of peaceful happiness ran a thread of care. One that cropped up in strange places, and disappeared again, but which left a quiet tone over the whole fabric–they had no child.

They had their share of sorrow, for when time was ripe
The still affection of the heart became an outward breathing type,
That into stillness passed again,
But left a want unknown before.

There was something simple and holy in their patient endurance of their lonely life–for lonely a house must ever be without children to those who love truly. Theirs was not the eager, disappointed longing of those whose union had proved fruitless. It was the simple, patient, hopeless resignation of those who find that a common sorrow draws them more closely together than many common joys. I myself could note the warmth of their hearts and their strong philoprogenitive feeling in their manner towards me.

From the time when I lay sick in college when Mrs Trevor appeared to my fever-dimmed eyes like an angel of mercy, I felt myself growing in their hearts. Who can imagine my gratitude to the lady who, merely because she heard of my sickness and desolation from a college friend, came and nursed me night and day till the fever left me. When I was sufficiently strong to be moved she had me brought away to the country, where good air, care, and attention soon made me stronger than ever. From that time I became a constant visitor at the Trevors' house; and as month after month rolled by I felt that I was growing in their affections. For four summers I spent my long vacation in their house, and each year I could feel Mr Trevor's shake of the hand grow heartier, and his wife's kiss on my forehead–for so she always saluted me–grow more tender and motherly.

Their liking for me had now grown so much that in their heart of hearts–and it was a sanctum common to them both–they secretly loved me as a son. Their love was returned manifold by the lonely boy, whose devotion to the kindest friends of his youth and his trouble had increased with his growth into manhood. Even in my own heart I was ashamed to confess how I loved them both–how I worshipped Mrs Trevor as I adored the mother whom I had lost so young, and whose eyes shone sometimes even then upon me, like stars, in my sleep.

It is strange how timorous we are when our affections are concerned. Merely because I had never told her how I loved her as a mother, because she had never told me how she loved me as a son, I used sometimes to think of her with a sort of lurking suspicion that I was trusting too much to my imagination. Sometimes even I would try to avoid thinking of her altogether, till my yearning would grow too strong to be repelled, and then I would think of her long and silently, and would love her more and more. My life was so lonely that I clung to her as the only thing I had to love. Of course I loved her husband, too, but I never thought about him in the same way; for men are less demonstrative about their affections to each other, and even acknowledge them to themselves less.

Mrs Trevor was an excellent hostess. She always let her guests see that they were welcome, and, unless in the case of casual visitors, that they were expected. She was, as may be imagined, very popular with all classes; but what is more rare, she was equally popular with both sexes. To be popular with her own sex is the touchstone of a woman's worth. To the houses of the peasantry she came, they said, like an angel, and brought comfort wherever she came. She knew the proper way to deal with the poor; she always helped them materially, but never offended their feelings in so doing. Young people all adored her.

My curiosity had been aroused as to the sort of place Scarp was; for, in order to give me a surprise, they would not tell me anything about it, but said that I must wait and judge it for myself. I had looked forward to my visit with both expectation and curiosity.

When I entered the hall, Mrs Trevor came out to welcome me and kissed me on the forehead, after her usual manner. Several of the old servants came near, smiling and bowing, and wishing welcome to 'Master Frank'. I shook hands with several of them, whilst their mistress looked on with a pleased smile.

As we went into a snug parlour, where a table was laid out with the materials for a comfortable supper, Mrs Trevor said to me: 'I am glad you came so soon, Frank. We have no one here at present, so you will be quite alone with us for a few days; and you will be quite alone with me this evening, for Charley is gone to a dinner party at Westholm.'

I told her that I was glad that there was no one else at Scarp, for that I would rather be with her and her husband than any one else in the world. She smiled as she said: 'Frank, if any one else said that, I would put it down as a mere compliment; but I know you always speak the truth. It is all very well to be alone with an old couple like Charley and me for two or three days; but just you wait till Thursday, and you will look on the intervening days as quite wasted.'

'Why?' I enquired.

'Because, Frank, there is a girl coming to stay with me then, with whom I intend you to fall in love.'

I answered jocosely: 'Oh, thank you, Mrs Trevor, very

much for your kind intentions–but suppose for a moment that they should be impracticable. "One man may lead a horse to the pond's brink." "The best laid schemes o' mice an' men." Eh?'

'Frank, don't be silly. I do not want to make you fall in love against your inclination; but I hope and I believe that you will.'

'Well, I'm sure I hope you won't be disappointed; but I never yet heard a person praised that I did not experience a disappointment when I came to know him or her.'

'Frank, did I praise any one?'

'Well, I am vain enough to think that your saying that you knew I would fall in love with her was a sort of indirect praise.'

'Dear, me, Frank, how modest you have grown.' A sort of indirect praise! 'Your humility is quite touching.'

'May I ask who the lady is, as I am supposed to be an interested party?'

'I do not know that I ought to tell you on account of your having expressed any doubt as to her merits. Besides, I might weaken the effect of the introduction. If I stimulate your curiosity it will be a point in my favour.'

'Oh, very well; I suppose I must only wait?'

'Ah, well, Frank, I will tell you. It is not fair to keep you waiting. She is a Miss Fothering.'

'Fothering? Fothering? I think I know that name. I remember hearing it somewhere, a long time ago, if I do not mistake. Where does she come from?'

'Her father is a clergyman in Norfolk, but he belongs to the Warwickshire family. I met her at Winthrop, Sir Harry Blount's place, a few months ago, and took a great liking for her, which she returned, and so we became fast friends. I made her promise to pay me a visit this summer, so she and her sister are coming here on Thursday to stay for some time.'

'And, may I be bold enough to enquire what she is like?'

'You may enquire if you like, Frank; but you won't get an answer. I shall not try to describe her. You must wait and judge for yourself.'

'Wait,' said I, 'three whole days? How can I do that? Do, tell me.'

She remained firm to her determination. I tried several times in the course of the evening to find out something more about Miss Fothering, for my curiosity was roused; but all the answer I could get on the subject was: 'Wait, Frank; wait, and judge for yourself.'

When I was bidding her good night, Mrs Trevor said to me: 'By the bye, Frank, you will have to give up the room which you will sleep in tonight, after tomorrow. I will have such a full house that I cannot let you have a doubled-bedded room all to yourself; so I will give that room to the Miss Fotherings, and move you up to the second floor. I just want you to see the room, as it has a romantic look about it, and has all the old furniture that was in it when we came here. There are several pictures in it worth looking at.'

My bedroom was a large chamber–immense for a bedroom–with two windows opening level with the floor, like those of the parlours and drawing-rooms. The furniture was old-fashioned, but not old enough to be curious, and on the walls hung many pictures–portraits–the house was full of portraits–and landscapes. I just glanced at these, intending to examine them in the morning, and went to bed. There was a fire in the room, and I lay awake for some time looking dreamily at the shadows of the furniture flitting over the walls and ceiling as the flames of the wood fire leaped and fell, and the red embers dropped whitening on the hearth. I tried to give the rein to my thoughts, but they kept constantly to the one subject–the mysterious Miss Fothering, with whom I was to fall in love. I was sure that I had heard her name somewhere, and I had at times lazy recollections of a child's face. At such times I would start awake from my growing drowsiness, but before I could collect my scattered thoughts the idea had eluded me. I could remember neither when nor where I had heard the name, nor could I recall even the expression of the child's face. It must have been long,

long ago, when I was young. When I was young my mother was alive. My mother–mother–mother. I found myself half awakening, and repeating the word over and over again. At last I fell asleep.

I thought that I awoke suddenly to that peculiar feeling which we sometimes have on starting from sleep, as if some one had been speaking in the room, and the voice is still echoing through it. All was quite silent, and the fire had gone out. I looked out of the window that lay straight opposite the foot of the bed, and observed a light outside, which gradually grew brighter till the room was almost as light as by day. The window looked like a picture in the framework formed by the cornice over the foot of the bed, and the massive pillars shrouded in curtains which supported it.

With the new accession of light I looked round the room, but nothing was changed. All was as before, except that some of the objects of furniture and ornament were shown in stronger relief than hitherto. Amongst these, those most in relief were the other bed, which was placed across the room, and an old picture that hung on the wall at its foot. As the bed was merely the counterpart of the one in which I lay, my attention became fixed on the picture. I observed it closely and with great interest. It seemed old, and was the portrait of a young girl, whose face, though kindly and merry, bore signs of thought and a capacity for deep feeling–

almost for passion. At some moments, as I looked at it, it called up before my mind a vision of Shakespeare's Beatrice, and once I thought of Beatrice Cenci. But this was probably caused by the association of ideas suggested by the similarity of names.

The light in the room continued to grow even brighter, so I looked again out of the window to seek its source, and saw there a lovely sight. It seemed as if there were grouped without the window three lovely children, who seemed to float in midair. The light seemed to spring from a point far behind them, and by their side was something dark and shadowy, which served to set off their radiance.

The children seemed to be smiling in upon something in the room, and, following their glances, I saw that their eyes rested upon the other bed. There, strange to say, the head which I had lately seen in the picture rested upon the pillow. I looked at the wall, but the frame was empty, the picture was gone. Then I looked at the bed again, and saw the young girl asleep, with the expression of her face constantly changing, as though she were dreaming.

As I was observing her, a sudden look of terror spread over her face, and she sat up like a sleepwalker, with her eyes wide open, staring out of the window.

Again turning to the window, my gaze became fixed, for a great and weird change had taken place. The figures were still there, but their features and expressions had become woefully different. Instead of the happy innocent look of childhood was one of malignity. With the change the children had grown old, and now three hags, decrepit and deformed, like typical witches, were before me.

But a thousand times worse than this transformation was the change in the dark mass that was near them. From a cloud, misty and undefined, it became a sort of shadow with a form. This gradually, as I looked, grew darker and fuller, till at length it made me shudder. There stood before me the phantom of the Fiend.

There was a long period of dead silence, in which I could hear the beating of my heart; but at length the phantom spoke to the others. His words seemed to issue from his lips mechanically, and without expression: 'Tomorrow, and tomorrow, and tomorrow. The fairest and the best.' He looked so awful that the question arose in my mind: 'Would I dare to face him without the window—would any one dare to go amongst those fiends?' A harsh, strident, diabolical laugh from without seemed to answer my unasked question in the negative.

But as well as the laugh I heard another sound—the tones of a sweet sad voice in despair coming across the room.

'Oh, alone, alone! is there no human thing near me? No hope—no hope. I shall go mad—or die.'

The last words were spoken with a gasp.

I tried to jump out of bed, but could not stir, my limbs were bound in sleep. The young girl's head fell suddenly back upon the pillow, and the limp-hanging jaw and wide-open, purposeless mouth spoke but too plainly of what had happened.

Again I heard from without the fierce, diabolical laughter, which swelled louder and louder, till at last it grew so strong that in very horror I shook aside my sleep and sat up in bed. I listened and heard a knocking at the door, but in another moment I became more awake, and knew that the sound came from the hall. It was, no doubt, Mr Trevor returning from his party.

The hall door was opened and shut, and then came a subdued sound of tramping and voices, but this soon died away, and there was silence throughout the house.

I lay awake for long thinking, and looking across the room at the picture and at the empty bed; for the moon now shone brightly, and the night was rendered still brighter by occasional flashes of summer lightning. At times the silence was broken by an owl screeching outside.

As I lay awake, pondering, I was very much troubled by what I had seen; but at length, putting several things together, I came to the conclusion that I had had a dream of a kind that might have been expected. The lightning, the knocking at the hall door, the screeching of the owl, the empty bed, and the face in the picture, when grouped together, supplied materials for the main facts of the vision. The rest was, of course, the offspring of pure fancy, and the natural consequence of the component elements mentioned acting with each other in the mind.

I got up and looked out of the window, but saw nothing but the broad belt of moonlight glittering on the bosom of the lake, which extended miles and miles away, till its farther shore was lost in the night haze, and the green sward, dotted with shrubs and tall grasses, which lay between the lake and the house.

The vision had utterly faded. However, the dream—for so, I suppose, I should call it—was very powerful, and I slept no more till the sunlight was streaming broadly in at the window, and then I fell into a doze.

2

MORE LINKS

Late in the morning I was awakened by Parks, Mr Trevor's man, who always used to attend on me when I visited my friends. He brought me hot water and the local news; and, chatting with him, I forgot for a time my alarm of the night.

Parks was staid and elderly, and a type of a class now rapidly disappearing—the class of old family servants who are as proud of their hereditary loyalty to their masters, as those masters are of name and rank. Like all old servants he had a great loving for all sorts of traditions. He believed them, and feared them, and had the most profound reverence for anything which had a story.

I asked him if he knew anything of the legendary history of Scarp. He answered with an air of doubt and hesitation, as of one carefully delivering an opinion which was still incomplete.

'Well, you see, Master Frank, that Scarp is so old that it must have any number of legends; but it is so long since it was inhabited that no one in the village remembers them.

The place seems to have become in a kind of way forgotten, and died out of people's thoughts, and so I am very much afraid, sir, that all the genuine history is lost.'

'What do you mean by the genuine history?' I enquired.

'Well, sir, I mean the true tradition, and not the inventions of the village folk. I heard the sexton tell some stories, but I am quite sure that they were not true, for I could see, Master Frank, that he did not believe them himself, but was only trying to frighten us.'

'And could you not hear of any story that appeared to you to be true?'

'No, sir, and I tried very hard. You see, Master Frank, that there is a sort of club held every week in the tavern down in the village, composed of very respectable men, sir–very respectable men, indeed–and they asked me to be their chairman. I spoke to the master about it, and he gave me leave to accept their proposal. I accepted it as they made a point of it; and from my position I have of course a fine opportunity of making enquiries. It was at the club, sir, that I was, last night, so that I was not here to attend on you, which I hope that you will excuse.'

Parks's air of mingled pride and condescension, as he made the announcement of the club, was very fine, and the effect was heightened by the confiding frankness with which he spoke. I asked him if he could find no clue to any of the legends which must have existed about such an old place. He answered with a very slight reluctance: 'Well, sir, there was one woman in the village who was awfully old and doting, and she evidently knew something about Scarp, for when she heard the name she mumbled out something about "awful stories" and "times of horror", and such like things, but I couldn't make her understand what it was I wanted to know, or keep her up to the point.'

'And have you tried often, Parks? Why do you not try again?'

'She is dead, sir!'

I had felt inclined to laugh at Parks when he was telling me of the old woman. The way in which he gloated over the words 'awful stories', and 'times of horror', was beyond the power of description; it should have been heard and seen to have been properly appreciated. His voice became deep and mysterious, and he almost smacked his lips at the thought of so much pabulum for nightmares. But when he calmly told me that the woman was dead, a sense of blankness, mingled with awe, came upon me. Here, the last link between myself and the mysterious past was broken, never to be mended. All the rich stores of legend and tradition that had arisen from strange conjunctures of circumstances, and from the belief and imagination of long lines of villagers, loyal to their suzerain lord, were lost forever. I felt quite sad and disappointed; and no attempt was made either by Parks or myself to continue the conversation. Mr Trevor came presently into my room, and having greeted each other warmly we went together to breakfast.

At breakfast Mrs Trevor asked me what I thought of the girl's portrait in my bedroom. We had often had discussions as to characters in faces for we were both physiognomists, and she asked the question as if she were really curious to hear my opinion. I told her that I had only seen it for a short time, and so would rather not attempt to give a final opinion without a more careful study; but from what I had seen of it I had been favourably impressed.

'Well, Frank, after breakfast go and look at it again carefully, and then tell me exactly what you think about it.'

After breakfast I did as directed and returned to the breakfast room, where Mrs Trevor was still sitting.

'Well, Frank, what is your opinion—mind, correctly. I want it for a particular reason.'

I told her what I thought of the girl's character; which, if there be any truth in physiognomy, must have been a very fine one.

'Then you like the face?'

I answered: 'It is a great pity that we have none such nowadays. They seem to have died out with Sir Joshua and Greuze. If I could meet such a girl as I believe the prototype of that portrait to have been I would never be happy till I had made her my wife.'

To my intense astonishment my hostess jumped up and clapped her hands. I asked her why she did it, and she laughed as she replied in a mocking tone imitating my own voice: 'But suppose for a moment that your kind intentions should be frustrated. "One man may lead a horse to the pond's brink." "The best laid schemes o' mice an' men." Eh?'

'Well,' said I, 'there may be some point in the observation. I suppose there must be since you have made it. But for my part I don't see it.'

'Oh, I forgot to tell you, Frank, that that portrait might have been painted for Diana Fothering.'

I felt a blush stealing over my face. She observed it and took my hand between hers as we sat down on the sofa, and said to me tenderly: 'Frank, my dear boy, I intend to jest with you no more on the subject. I have a conviction that you will like Diana, which has been strengthened by your admiration for her portrait, and from what I know of human nature I am sure that she will like you. Charley and I both wish to see you married, and we would not think of a wife for you who was not in every way eligible. I have never in my life met a girl like Di; and if you and she fancy each other it will be Charley's pleasure and my own to enable you to marry—as far as means are concerned. Now, don't speak. You must know perfectly well how much we both love you. We have always regarded you as our son, and we intend to treat you as our only child when it pleases God to separate us. There now, think the matter over, after you have seen Diana. But, mind me, unless you love each other well and truly, we would far rather not see you married. At all events, whatever may happen you have our best wishes and prayers for your happiness. God bless you, Frank, my dear, dear boy.'

There were tears in her eyes as she spoke. When she had finished she leaned over, drew down my head and kissed my forehead very, very tenderly, and then got up softly and left the room. I felt inclined to cry myself. Her words to me were tender, and sensible, and womanly, but I cannot attempt to describe the infinite tenderness and gentleness of her voice and manner. I prayed for every blessing on her in my secret heart, and the swelling of my throat did not prevent my prayers finding voice. There may have been women in the world like Mrs Trevor, but if there had been I had never met any of them, except herself.

As may be imagined, I was most anxious to see Miss Fothering, and for the remainder of the day she was constantly in my thoughts. That evening a letter came from the younger Miss Fothering apologising for her not being able to keep her promise with reference to her visit, on account of the unexpected arrival of her aunt, with whom she was obliged to go to Paris for some months. That night I slept in my new room, and had neither dream nor vision. I awoke in the morning half ashamed of having ever paid any attention to such a silly circumstance as a strange dream in my first night in an old house.

After breakfast next morning, as I was going along the corridor, I saw the door of my old bedroom open, and went in to have another look at the portrait. Whilst I was looking at it I began to wonder how it could be that it was so like Miss Fothering as Mrs Trevor said it was. The more I thought of this the more it puzzled me, till suddenly the dream came back–the face in the picture, and the figure in the bed, the phantoms out in the night, and the ominous words: 'The fairest and the best'. As I thought of these things all the possibilities of the lost legends of the old house thronged so quickly into my mind that I began to feel a buzzing in my ears and my head began to swim, so that I was obliged to sit down.

'Could it be possible,' I asked myself, 'that some old curse hangs over the race that once dwelt within these walls, and can she be of that race? Such things have been before now!'

The idea was a terrible one for me, for it made to me a reality that which I had come to look upon as merely the dream of a distempered imagination. If the thought had come to me in the darkness and stillness of the night it would have been awful. How happy I was that it had come by daylight, when the sun was shining brightly, and the air was cheerful with the trilling of the song birds, and the lively, strident cawing from the old rookery.

I stayed in the room for some little time longer, thinking over the scene, and, as is natural, when I had got over the remnants of my fear, my reason began to question the genuineness of the dream. I began to look for the internal evidence of the untruth to facts; but, after thinking earnestly for some time the only fact that seemed to me of any importance was the confirmatory one of the younger Miss Fothering's apology. In the dream the frightened girl had been alone, and the mere fact of two girls coming on a visit had seemed a sort of disproof of its truth. But, just as if things were conspiring to force on the truth of the dream, one of the sisters was not to come, and the other was she who resembled the portrait whose prototype I had seen sleeping in a vision. I could hardly imagine that I had only dreamt.

I determined to ask Mrs Trevor if she could explain in any way Miss Fothering's resemblance to the portrait, and so went at once to seek her.

I found her in the large drawing room alone, and, after a few casual remarks, I broached the subject on which I had come to seek for information. She had not said anything further to me about marrying since our conversation on the previous day, but when I mentioned Miss Fothering's name I could see a glad look on her face which gave me great pleasure. She made none of those vulgar commonplace remarks which many women find it necessary to make when talking to a man about a girl for whom he is supposed to have an affection, but by her manner she put me entirely at my ease, as I sat fidgeting on the sofa, pulling purposelessly the woolly tufts of an antimacassar, painfully conscious that my cheeks were red, and my voice slightly forced and unnatural.

She merely said, 'Of course, Frank, I am ready if you want to talk about Miss Fothering, or any other subject.' She then put a marker in her book and laid it aside, and, folding her arms, looked at me with a grave, kind, expectant smile.

I asked her if she knew anything about the family history of Miss Fothering. She answered: 'Not further than I have already told you. Her father's is a fine old family, although reduced in circumstances.'

'Has it ever been connected with any family in this county? With the former owners of Scarp, for instance?'

'Not that I know of. Why do you ask?'

'I want to find out how she comes to be so like that portrait.'

'I never thought of that. It may be that there was some remote connection between her family and the Kirks who formerly owned Scarp. I will ask her when she comes. Or stay. Let us go and look if there is any old book or tree in the library that will throw a light upon the subject. We have rather a good library now, Frank, for we have all our own books, and all those which belonged to the Scarp library also. They are in great disorder, for we have been waiting till you came to arrange them, for we knew that you delighted in such work.'

'There is nothing I should enjoy more than arranging all these splendid books. What a magnificent library. It is almost a pity to keep it in a private house.'

We proceeded to look for some of those old books of family history which are occasionally to be found in old county houses. The library of Scarp, I saw, was very valuable, and as we prosecuted our search I came across many splendid and rare volumes which I determined to examine at my leisure, for I had come to Scarp for a long visit.

We searched first in the old folio shelves, and, after some few disappointments, found at length a large volume, magnificently printed and bound, which contained views and plans of the house, illuminations of the armorial bearings of the family of Kirk, and all the families with whom it was connected, and having the history of all these families carefully set forth. It was called on the title page 'The Book of Kirk', and was full of anecdotes and legends, and contained a large stock of family tradition. As this was exactly the book which we required, we searched no further, but, having carefully dusted the volume, bore it to Mrs Trevor's boudoir where we could look over it quite undisturbed.

On looking in the index, we found the name of Fothering mentioned, and on turning to the page specified, found the arms of Kirk quartered on those of Fothering. From the text we learned that one of the daughters of Kirk had, in the year 1573, married the brother of Fothering against the united wills of her father and brother, and that after a bitter feud of some ten or twelve years, the latter, then master of Scarp, had met the brother of Fothering in a duel and had killed him. Upon receiving the news Fothering had sworn a great oath to revenge his brother, invoking the most fearful curses upon himself and his race if he should fail to cut off the hand that had slain his brother, and to nail it over the gate of Fothering. The feud then became so bitter that Kirk seems to have gone quite mad on the subject. When he heard of Fothering's oath he knew that he had but little chance of escape, since his enemy was his master at every weapon; so he determined upon a mode of revenge which, although costing him his own life, he fondly hoped would accomplish the eternal destruction of his brother-in-law through his violated oath. He sent Fothering a letter cursing him and his race, and praying for the consummation of his own curse invoked in case of failure. He concluded his missive by a prayer for the complete destruction; soul, mind, and body, of the first Fothering who should enter the gate of Scarp, who he hoped would be the fairest and best of the race. Having despatched this letter he cut off his right hand and threw it into the centre of a roaring fire, which he had made for the purpose. When it was entirely consumed he threw himself upon his sword, and so died.

A cold shiver went through me when I read the words 'fairest and best'. All my dream came back in a moment, and I seemed to hear in my ears again the echo of the fiendish laughter. I looked up at Mrs Trevor, and saw that she had become very grave. Her face had a half-frightened look, as if some wild thought had struck her. I was more frightened than ever, for nothing increases our alarms so much as the sympathy of others with regard to them; however, I tried to conceal my fear. We sat silent for some minutes, and then Mrs Trevor rose up saying: 'Come with me, and let us look at the portrait.'

I remember her saying *the* and not *that* portrait, as if some concealed thought of it had been occupying her mind. The same dread had assailed her from a coincidence as had grown in me from a vision. Surely–surely I had good grounds for fear!

We went to the bedroom and stood before the picture,

which seemed to gaze upon us with an expression which reflected our own fears. My companion said to me in slightly excited tones: 'Frank, lift down the picture till we see its back.' I did so, and we found written in strange old writing on the grimy canvas a name and a date, which, after a great deal of trouble, we made out to be 'Margaret Kirk, 1572'. It was the name of the lady in the book.

Mrs Trevor turned round and faced me slowly, with a look of horror on her face.

'Frank, I don't like this at all. There is something very strange here.'

I had it on my tongue to tell her my dream, but was ashamed to do so. Besides, I feared that it might frighten her too much, as she was already alarmed.

I continued to look at the picture as a relief from my embarrassment, and was struck with the excessive griminess of the back in comparison to the freshness of the front. I mentioned my difficulty to my companion, who thought for a moment, and then suddenly said: 'I see how it is. It has been turned with its face to the wall.'

I said no word but hung up the picture again; and we went back to the boudoir.

On the way I began to think that my fears were too wildly improbable to bear to be spoken about. It was so hard to believe in the horrors of darkness when the sunlight was falling brightly around me. The same idea seemed to have struck Mrs Trevor, for she said, when we entered the room: 'Frank, it strikes me that we are both rather silly to let our imaginations carry us away so. The story is merely a tradition, and we know how report distorts even the most innocent facts. It is true that the Fothering family was formerly connected with the Kirks, and that the picture is that of the Miss Kirk who married against her father's will; it is likely that he quarrelled with her for so doing, and had her picture turned to the wall–a common trick of angry fathers at all times–but that is all. There can be nothing beyond that. Let us not think any more upon the subject, as it is one likely to lead us into absurdities. However, the picture is a really beautiful one–independent of its being such a likeness of Diana, and I will have it placed in the dining-room.'

The change was effected that afternoon, but she did not again allude to the subject. She appeared, when talking to me, to be a little constrained in manner–a very unusual thing with her, and seemed to fear that I would renew the forbidden topic. I think that she did not wish to let her imagination lead her astray, and was distrustful of herself. However, the feeling of constraint wore off before night–but she did not renew the subject.

I slept well that night, without dreams of any kind; and next morning–the third tomorrow promised in the dream–

when I came down to breakfast, I was told that I would see Miss Fothering before that evening.

I could not help blushing, and stammered out some commonplace remark, and then glancing up, feeling very sheepish, I saw my hostess looking at me with her kindly smile intensified. She said: 'Do you know, Frank, I felt quite frightened yesterday when we were looking at the picture; but I have been thinking the matter over since, and have come to the conclusion that my folly was perfectly unfounded. I am sure you agree with me. In fact, I look now upon our fright as a good joke, and will tell it to Diana when she arrives.'

Once again I was about to tell my dream; but again was restrained by shame. I knew, of course, that Mrs Trevor would not laugh at me or even think little of me for my fears, for she was too well-bred, and kind-hearted, and sympathetic to do anything of the kind, and, besides, the fear was one which we had shared in common.

But how could I confess my fright at what might appear to others to be a ridiculous dream, when she had conquered the fear that had been common to us both, and which had arisen from a really strange conjuncture of facts. She appeared to look on the matter so lightly that I could not do otherwise. And I did it honestly for the time.

3

THE THIRD TOMORROW

In the afternoon I was out in the garden lying in the shadow of an immense beech, when I saw Mrs Trevor approaching. I had been reading Shelley's 'Stanzas Written in Dejection', and my heart was full of melancholy and a vague yearning after human sympathy. I had thought of Mrs Trevor's love for me, but even that did not seem sufficient. I wanted the love of some one more nearly of my own level, some equal spirit, for I looked on her, of course, as I would have regarded my mother. Somehow my thoughts kept returning to Miss Fothering till I could almost see her before me in my memory of the portrait. I had begun to ask myself the question: 'Are you in love?' when I heard the voice of my hostess as she drew near.

'Ha! Frank, I thought I would find you here. I want you to come to my boudoir.'

'What for?' I enquired, as I rose from the grass and picked up my volume of Shelley.

'Di has come ever so long ago; and I want to introduce you and have a chat before dinner,' said she, as we went towards the house.

'But won't you let me change my dress? I am not in correct costume for the afternoon.'

I felt somewhat afraid of the unknown beauty when the introduction was imminent. Perhaps it was because I had come to believe too firmly in Mrs Trevor's prediction.

'Nonsense, Frank, just as if any woman worth thinking about cares how a man is dressed.'

We entered the boudoir and found a young lady seated by a window that overlooked the croquet ground. She turned round as we came in, so Mrs Trevor introduced us, and we were soon engaged in a lively conversation. I observed her, as may be supposed, with more than curiosity, and shortly found that she was worth looking at. She was very beautiful, and her beauty lay not only in her features but in her expression. At first her appearance did not seem to me so perfect as it afterwards did, on account of her wonderful resemblance to the portrait with whose beauty I was already acquainted. But it was not long before I came to experience the difference between the portrait and the reality. No matter how well it may be painted a picture falls far short of its prototype. There is something in a real face which cannot exist on canvas–some difference far greater than that contained in the contrast between the one expression, however beautiful, of the picture, and the moving features and varying expression of the reality. There is something living and lovable in a real face that no art can represent.

When we had been talking for a while in the usual

conventional style, Mrs Trevor said, 'Di, my love, I want to tell you of a discovery Frank and I have made. You must know that I always call Mr Stanford, Frank–he is more like my own son than my friend, and that I am very fond of him.'

She then put her arms round Miss Fothering's waist, as they sat on the sofa together, and kissed her, and then, turning towards me, said, 'I don't approve of kissing girls in the presence of gentlemen, but you know that Frank is not supposed to be here. This is my sanctum, and who invades it must take the consequences. But I must tell you about the discovery.'

She then proceeded to tell the legend, and about her finding the name of Margaret Kirk on the back of the picture.

Miss Fothering laughed gleefully as she heard the story, and then said, suddenly, 'Oh, I had forgotten to tell you, dear Mrs Trevor, that I had such a fright the other day. I thought I was going to be prevented coming here. Aunt Deborah came to us last week for a few days, and when she heard that I was about to go on a visit to Scarp she seemed quite frightened, and went straight off to papa and asked him to forbid me to go. Papa asked her why she made the request, so she told a long family legend about any of us coming to Scarp–just the same story that you have been telling me. She said she was sure that some misfortune would happen if I came; so you see that the tradition exists in our branch of the family too. Oh, you can't fancy the scene there was between papa and Aunt Deborah. I must laugh whenever I think of it, although I did not laugh then, for I was greatly afraid that aunty would prevent me coming. Papa got very grave, and aunty thought she had carried her point when he said, in his dear, old, pompous manner, "Deborah, Diana has promised to pay Mrs Trevor, of Scarp, a visit, and, of course, must keep her engagement. And if it were for no other reason than the one you have just alleged, I would strain a point of convenience to have her go to Scarp. I have always educated my children in such a manner that they ought not to be influenced by such vain superstitions; and with my will their practice shall never be at variance with the precepts which I have instilled into them." Poor aunty was quite overcome. She seemed almost speechless for a time at the thought that her wishes had been neglected, for you know that Aunt Deborah's wishes are commands to all our family.'

Mrs Trevor said: 'I hope Mrs Howard was not offended?'

'Oh, no. Papa talked to her seriously, and at length–with a great deal of difficulty I must say–succeeded in convincing her that her fears were groundless–at least, he forced her to confess that such things as she was afraid of could not be.'

I thought of the couplet:

A   man   convinced   against   his   will

Is of the same opinion still

but said nothing.

Miss Fothering finished her story by saying: 'Aunty ended by hoping that I might enjoy myself, which I am sure, my dear Mrs Trevor, that I will do.'

'I hope you will, my love.'

I had been struck during the above conversation by the mention of Mrs Howard. I was trying to think of where I had heard the name, Deborah Howard, when suddenly it all came back to me. Mrs Howard had been Miss Fothering, and was an old friend of my mother's. It was thus that I had been accustomed to her name when I was a child. I remembered now that once she had brought a nice little girl, almost a baby, with her to visit. The child was her niece, and it was thus that I now accounted for my half-recollection of the name and the circumstance on the first night of my arrival at Scarp. The thought of my dream here recalled me to Mrs Trevor's object in bringing Miss Fothering to her boudoir, so I said to the latter: 'Do you believe these legends?'

'Indeed I do not, Mr Stanford; I do not believe in anything half so silly.'

'Then you do not believe in ghosts or visions?'

'Most certainly not.'

How could I tell my dream to a girl who had such profound disbelief? And yet I felt something whispering to me that I ought to tell it to her. It was, no doubt, foolish of me to have this fear of a dream, but I could not help it. I was just going to risk being laughed at, and unburden my mind, when Mrs Trevor started up, after looking at her watch, saying: 'Dear me, I never thought it was so late. I must go and see if any others have come. It will not do for me to neglect my guests.'

We all left the boudoir, and as we did so the gong sounded for dressing for dinner, and so we each sought our rooms.

When I came down to the drawing room I found assembled a number of persons who had arrived during the course of the afternoon. I was introduced to them all, and chatted with them till dinner was announced. I was given Miss Fothering to take into dinner, and when it was over I found that we had improved our acquaintance very much. She was a delightful girl, and as I looked at her I thought with a glow of pleasure of Mrs Trevor's prediction. Occasionally I saw our hostess observing us, and as she saw us chatting pleasantly together as though we enjoyed it a more than happy look came into her face. It was one of her most fascinating points that in the midst of gaiety, while she never neglected anyone, she specially remembered her particular friends. No matter what position she might be placed in she would still remember that there were some persons who would treasure up her recognition at such moments.

After dinner, as I did not feel inclined to enter the drawing room with the other gentlemen, I strolled out into the garden by myself, and thought over things in general, and Miss Fothering in particular. The subject was such a pleasant one that I quite lost myself in it, and strayed off farther than I had intended. Suddenly I remembered myself and looked around. I was far away from the house, and in the midst of a dark, gloomy walk between old yew trees. I could not see through them on either side on account of their thickness, and as the walk was curved I could see but a short distance either before or behind me. I looked up and saw a yellowish, luminous sky with heavy clouds passing sluggishly across it. The moon had not yet risen, and the general gloom reminded me forcibly of some of the weird pictures which William Blake so loved to paint. There was a sort of vague melancholy and ghostliness in the place that made me shiver, and I hurried on.

At length the walk opened and I came out on a large sloping lawn, dotted here and there with yew trees and tufts of pampas grass of immense height, whose stalks were crowned with large flowers. To the right lay the house, grim and gigantic in the gloom, and to the left the lake which stretched away so far that it was lost in the evening shadow. The lawn sloped from the terrace round the house down to the water's edge, and was only broken by the walk which continued to run on round the house in a wide sweep.

As I came near the house a light appeared in one of the windows which lay before me, and as I looked into the room I saw that it was the chamber of my dream.

Unconsciously I approached nearer and ascended the terrace, from the top of which I could see across the deep trench which surrounded the house, and looked earnestly into the room. I shivered as I looked. My spirits had been damped by the gloom and desolation of the yew walk, and now the dream and all the subsequent revelations came before my mind with such vividness that the horror of the thing again seized me, but more forcibly than before. I looked at the sleeping arrangements, and groaned as I saw that the bed where the dying woman had seemed to lie was alone prepared, while the other bed, that in which I had slept, had its curtains drawn all round. This was but another link in the chain of doom. Whilst I stood looking, the servant who was in the room came and pulled down one of the blinds, but, as she was about to do the same with the other, Miss Fothering entered the room, and, seeing what she was about, evidently gave her contrary directions, for she let go the window string, and then went and pulled up again the blind which she had let down. Having done so she followed her mistress out of the room. So wrapped up was I in all that took place with reference to that chamber, that it never even struck me that I was guilty of any impropriety in watching what took place.

I stayed there for some little time longer purposeless and terrified. The horror grew so great to me as I thought of the events of the last few days, that I determined to tell Miss Fothering of my dream, in order that she might not be frightened in case she should see anything like it, or at least that she might be prepared for anything that might happen. As soon as I had come to this determination the inevitable question 'when?' presented itself. The means of making the communication was a subject most disagreeable to contemplate, but as I had made up my mind to do it, I thought that there was no time like the present. Accordingly I was determined to seek the drawing room, where I knew I should find Miss Fothering and Mrs Trevor, for, of course, I had determined to take the latter into our confidence. As I was really afraid to go through the awful yew walk again, I completed the half circle of the house and entered the backdoor, from which I easily found my way to the drawing room.

When I entered Mrs Trevor, who was sitting near the door, said to me, 'Good gracious, Frank, where have you been to make you look so pale? One would think you had seen a ghost!'

I answered that I had been strolling in the garden, but

made no other remark, as I did not wish to say anything about my dream before the persons to whom she was talking, as they were strangers to me. I waited for some time for an opportunity of speaking to her alone, but her duties, as hostess, kept her so constantly occupied that I waited in vain. Accordingly I determined to tell Miss Fothering at all events, at once, and then to tell Mrs Trevor as soon as an opportunity for doing so presented itself.

With a good deal of difficulty–for I did not wish to do anything marked–I succeeded in getting Miss Fothering away from the persons by whom she was surrounded, and took her to one of the embrasures, under the pretence of looking out at the night view. Here we were quite removed from observation, as the heavy window curtains completely covered the recess, and almost isolated us from the rest of the company as perfectly as if we were in a separate chamber. I proceeded at once to broach the subject for which I had sought the interview; for I feared lest contact with the lively company of the drawing room would do away with my present fears, and so break down the only barrier that stood between her and Fate.

'Miss Fothering, do you ever dream?'

'Oh, yes, often. But I generally find that my dreams are most ridiculous.'

'How so?'

'Well, you see, that no matter whether they are good or bad they appear real and coherent whilst I am dreaming them; but when I wake I find them unreal and incoherent, when I remember them at all. They are, in fact, mere disconnected nonsense.'

'Are you fond of dreams?'

'Of course I am. I delight in them, for whether they are sense or gibberish when you wake, they are real whilst you are asleep.'

'Do you believe in dreams?'

'Indeed, Mr Stanford, I do not.'

'Do you like hearing them told?'

'I do, very much, when they are worth telling. Have you been dreaming anything? If you have, do tell it to me.'

'I will be glad to do so. It is about a dream which I had that concerns you, that I came here to tell you.'

'About me. Oh, how nice. Do go on.'

I told her all my dream, after calling her attention to our conversation in the boudoir as a means of introducing the subject. I did not attempt to heighten the effect in any way or to draw any inferences. I tried to suppress my own emotion and merely to let the facts speak for themselves. She listened with great eagerness, but, as far as I could see, without a particle of either fear or belief in the dream as a warning. When I had finished she laughed a quiet, soft laugh, and said: 'That is delicious. And was I really the girl that you saw afraid of ghosts? If papa heard of such a thing as that even in a dream what a lecture he would give me! I wish I could dream anything like that.'

'Take care,' said I, 'you might find it too awful. It might indeed prove the fulfilling of the ban which we saw in the legend in the old book, and which you heard from your aunt.'

She laughed musically again, and shook her head at me wisely and warningly.

'Oh, pray do not talk nonsense and try to frighten me—for I warn you that you will not succeed.'

'I assure you on my honour, Miss Fothering, that I was never more in earnest in my whole life.'

'Do you not think that we had better go into the room?' said she, after a few moments' pause.

'Stay just a moment, I entreat you,' said I. 'What I say is true. I am really in earnest.'

'Oh, pray forgive me if what I said led you to believe that I doubted your word. It was merely your inference which I disagreed with. I thought you had been jesting to try and frighten me.'

'Miss Fothering, I would not presume to take such a liberty. But I am glad that you trust me. May I venture to ask you a favour? Will you promise me one thing?'

Her answer was characteristic: 'No. What is it?'

'That you will not be frightened at anything which may take place tonight?'

She laughed softly again.

'I do not intend to be. But is that all?'

'Yes, Miss Fothering, that is all; but I want to be assured that you will not be alarmed—that you will be prepared for anything which may happen. I have a horrid foreboding of evil—some evil that I dread to think of—and it will be a great comfort to me if you will do one thing.'

'Oh, nonsense. Oh, well, if you really wish it I will tell you if I will do it when I hear what it is.'

Her levity was all gone when she saw how terribly in earnest I was. She looked at me boldly and fearlessly, but with a tender, half-pitying glance as if conscious of the possession of strength superior to mine. Her fearlessness was in her free, independent attitude, but her pity was in her eyes. I went on: 'Miss Fothering, the worst part of my dream was seeing the look of agony on the face of the girl when she looked round and found herself alone. Will you take some token and keep it with you till morning to remind you, in case anything should happen, that you are not alone—that there is one thinking of you, and one human intelligence awake for you, though all the rest of the world should be asleep or dead?'

In my excitement I spoke with fervour, for the possibility of her enduring the horror which had assailed me seemed to be growing more and more each instant. At times since that awful night I had disbelieved the existence of the warning, but when I thought of it by night I could not but believe, for the very air in the darkness seemed to be peopled by phantoms to my fevered imagination. My belief had been perfected tonight by the horror of the yew walk, and all the sombre, ghostly thoughts that had arisen amid its gloom.

There was a short pause. Miss Fothering leaned on the edge of the window, looking out at the dark, moonless sky. At length she turned and said to me, with some hesitation, 'But really, Mr Stanford, I do not like doing anything from fear of supernatural things, or from a belief in them. What you want me to do is so simple a thing in itself that I would not hesitate a moment to do it, but that papa has always taught me to believe that such occurrences as you seem to dread are quite impossible, and I know that he would be very much displeased if any act of mine showed a belief in them.'

'Miss Fothering, I honestly think that there is not a man living who would wish less than I would to see you or anyone else disobeying a father either in word or spirit, and more particularly when that father is a clergyman; but I entreat you to gratify me on this one point. It cannot do you any harm;

and I assure you that if you do not I will be inexpressibly miserable. I have endured the greatest tortures of suspense for the last three days, and tonight I feel a nervous horror of which words can give you no conception. I know that I have not the smallest right to make the request, and no reason for doing it except that I was fortunate, or unfortunate, enough to get the warning. I apologise most sincerely for the great liberty which I have taken, but believe me that I act with the best intentions.'

My excitement was so great that my knees were trembling, and large drops of perspiration rolling down my face.

There was a long pause, and I had almost made up my mind for a refusal of my request when my companion spoke again.

'Mr Stanford, on that plea alone I will grant your request. I can see that for some reason which I cannot quite comprehend you are deeply moved; and that I may be the means of saving pain to any one, I will do what you ask. Just please to state what you wish me to do.'

I thought from her manner that she was offended with me; however I explained my purpose: 'I want you to keep about you, when you go to bed, some token which will remind you in an instant of what has passed between us, so that you may not feel lonely or frightened–no matter what may happen.'

'I will do it. What shall I take?'

47

She had her handkerchief in her hand as she spoke. So I put my hand upon it and blessed it in the name of the Father, Son, and Holy Ghost. I did this to fix its existence in her memory by awing her slightly about it. 'This,' said I, 'shall be a token that you are not alone.' My object in blessing the handkerchief was fully achieved, for she did seem somewhat awed, but still she thanked me with a sweet smile. 'I feel that you act from your heart,' said she, 'and my heart thanks you.' She gave me her hand as she spoke, in an honest, straightforward manner, with more the independence of a man than the timorousness of a woman. As I grasped it I felt the blood rushing to my face, but before I let it go an impulse seized me and I bent down and touched it with my lips. She drew it quickly away, and said more coldly than she had yet spoken: 'I did not mean you to do that.'

'Believe me I did not mean to take a liberty–it was merely the natural expression of my gratitude. I feel as if you had done me some great personal service. You do not know how much lighter my heart is now than it was an hour ago, or you would forgive me for having so offended.'

As I made my apologetic excuse, I looked at her wistfully. She returned my glance fearlessly, but with a bright, forgiving smile. She then shook her head slightly, as if to banish the subject.

There was a short pause, and then she said: 'I am glad to

be of any service to you; but if there be any possibility of what you fear happening it is I who will be benefited. But mind, I will depend upon you not to say a word of this to anybody. I am afraid that we are both very foolish.'

'No, no, Miss Fothering. I may be foolish, but you are acting nobly in doing what seems to you to be foolish in order that you may save me from pain. But may I not even tell Mrs Trevor?'

'No, not even her. I should be ashamed of myself if I thought that anyone except ourselves knew about it.'

'You may depend upon me. I will keep it secret if you wish.'

'Do so, until morning at all events. Mind, if I laugh at you then I will expect you to join in my laugh.'

'I will,' said I. 'I will be only too glad to be able to laugh at it.' And we joined the rest of the company.

When I retired to my bedroom that night I was too much excited to sleep–even had my promise not forbidden me to do so. I paced up and down the room for some time, thinking and doubting. I could not believe completely in what I expected to happen, and yet my heart was filled with a vague dread. I thought over the events of the evening–particularly my stroll after dinner through that awful yew walk and my looking into the bedroom where I had dreamed. From these my thoughts wandered to the deep embrasure of the window where I had given Miss Fothering the token. I could hardly realise that whole interview as a fact. I knew that it had taken place, but that was all. It was so strange to recall a scene that, now that it was enacted, seemed half comedy and half tragedy, and to remember that it was played in this practical nineteenth century, in secret, within earshot of a room full of people, and only hidden from them by a curtain. I felt myself blushing, half from excitement, half from shame, when I thought of it. But then my thoughts turned to the way in which Miss Fothering had acceded to my request, strange as it was; and as I thought of her my blundering shame changed to a deeper glow of hope. I remembered Mrs Trevor's prediction—'From what I know of human nature I think that she will like you'—and as I did so I felt how dear to me Miss Fothering was already becoming. But my joy was turned to anger on thinking what she might be called on to endure; and the thought of her suffering pain or fright caused me greater distress than any suffered myself. Again my thoughts flew back to the time of my own fright and my dream, with all the subsequent revelations concerning it, rushed across my mind. I felt again the feeling of extreme terror—as if something was about to happen—as if the tragedy was approaching its climax. Naturally I thought of the time of night and so I looked at my watch. It was within a few minutes of one o'clock. I remembered that the clock had struck twelve after Mr Trevor had come home on the night of my dream. There was a large clock at Scarp which tolled the hours so loudly that for a long way round the estate the country people all regulated their affairs by it. The next few minutes passed so slowly that each moment seemed an age.

I was standing, with my watch in my hand, counting the moments when suddenly a light came into the room that made the candle on the table appear quite dim, and my shadow was reflected on the wall by some brilliant light which streamed in through the window. My heart for an instant ceased to beat, and then the blood rushed so violently to my temples that my eyes grew dim and my brain began to reel. However, I shortly became more composed, and then went to the window expecting to see my dream again repeated.

The light was there as formerly, but there were no figures of children, or witches, or fiends. The moon had just risen, and I could see its reflection upon the far end of the lake. I turned my head in trembling expectation to the ground below where I had seen the children and the hags, but saw merely the dark yew trees and tall crested pampas tufts gently moving in the night wind. The light caught the edges of the flowers of the grass, and made them most conspicuous.

As I looked a sudden thought flashed like a flame of fire through my brain. I saw in one second of time all the folly of my wild fancies. The moonlight and its reflection on the water shining into the room was the light of my dream, or phantasm as I now understood it to be. Those three tufts of pampas grass clumped together were in turn the fair young children and the withered leaves and the dark foliage of the yew beside them gave substance to the semblance of the fiend. For the rest, the empty bed and the face of the picture, my half-recollection of the name of Fothering, and the long-forgotten legend of the curse. Oh, fool! fool that I had been! How I had been the victim of circumstances, and of my own wild imagination! Then came the bitter reflection of the agony of mind which Miss Fothering might be compelled to suffer. Might not the recital of my dream, and my strange request regarding the token, combined with the natural causes of night and scene, produce the very effect which I so dreaded? It was only at that bitter, bitter moment that I realised how foolish I had been. But what was my anguish of mind to hers? For an instant I conceived the idea of rousing Mrs Trevor and telling her all the facts of the case so that she might go to Miss Fothering and tell her not to be alarmed. But I had no time to act upon my thought. As I was hastening to the door the clock struck one and a moment later I heard from the room below me a sharp scream—a cry of surprise rather than fear. Miss Fothering had no doubt been awakened by the striking of the clock, and had seen outside the window the very figures which I had described to her.

I rushed madly down the stairs and arrived at the door of her bedroom, which was directly under the one which I now occupied. As I was about to rush in I was instinctively restrained from so doing by the thoughts of propriety; and so for a few moments I stood silent, trembling, with my hand upon the door handle.

Within I heard a voice–her voice–exclaiming, in tones of stupefied surprise: 'Has it come then? Am I alone?' She then continued joyously, 'No, I am not alone. His token! Oh, thank God for that. Thank God for that.'

Through my heart at her words came a rush of wild delight. I felt my bosom swell and the tears of gladness spring to my eyes. In that moment I knew that I had strength and courage to face the world, alone, for her sake. But before my hopes had time to manifest themselves they were destroyed, for again the voice came wailing from the room of blank despair that made me cold from head to foot.

'Ah–h–h! still there? Oh! God, preserve my reason. Oh! for some human thing near me.' Then her voice changed slightly to a tone of entreaty: 'You will not leave me alone? Your token. Remember your token. Help me. Help me now.' Then her voice became more wild, and rose to an inarticulate, wailing scream of horror.

As I heard that agonised cry, I realised the idea that it was madness to delay–that I had hesitated too long already–I must cast aside the shackles of conventionality if I wished to repair my fatal error. Nothing could save her from some serious injury–perhaps madness–perhaps death; save a shock which would break the spell which was over her from fear and her excited imagination. I flung open the door and rushed in, shouting loudly: 'Courage, courage. You are not alone. I am here. Remember the token.'

She grasped the handkerchief instinctively, but she hardly comprehended my words, and did not seem to heed my presence. She was sitting up in bed, her face being distorted with terror, and was gazing out upon the scene. I heard from without the hooting of an owl as it flew across the border of the lake. She heard it also, and screamed: 'The laugh, too! Oh, there is no hope. Even he will not dare to go amongst them.'

Then she gave vent to a scream, so wild, so appalling that, as I heard it, I trembled, and the hair on the back of my head bristled up. Throughout the house I could hear screams of affright, and the ringing of bells, and the banging of doors, and the rush of hurried feet; but the poor sufferer comprehended not these sounds; she still continued gazing out of the window awaiting the consummation of the dream.

I saw that the time for action and self-sacrifice was come.

There was but one way now to repair my fatal error. To burst through the window and try by the shock to wake her from her trance of fear.

I said no word but rushed across the room and hurled myself, back foremost, against the massive plate glass. As I turned I saw Mrs Trevor rushing into the room, her face wild with excitement. She was calling out: 'Diana, Diana, what is it?'

The glass crashed and shivered into a thousand pieces, and I could feel its sharp edges cutting me like so many knives. But I heeded not the pain, for above the rushing of feet and crashing of glass and the shouting both within and without the room I heard her voice ring forth in a joyous, fervent cry, 'Saved. He has dared,' as she sank down in the arms of Mrs Trevor, who had thrown herself upon the bed.

Then I felt a mighty shock, and all the universe seemed filled with sparks of fire that whirled around me with lightning speed, till I seemed to be in the centre of a world of flame, and then came in my ears the rushing of a mighty wind, swelling ever louder, and then came a blackness over all things and a deadness of sound as if all the earth had passed away, and I remembered no more.

4

AFTERWARDS

When I next became conscious I was lying in bed in a dark room. I wondered what this was for, and tried to look around me, but could hardly stir my head. I attempted to speak, but my voice was without power—it was like a whisper from another world. The effort to speak made me feel faint, and again I felt a darkness gathering round me.

*   *   *

I became gradually conscious of something cool on my forehead. I wondered what it was. All sorts of things I conjectured, but could not fix my mind on any of them. I lay thus for some time, and at length opened my eyes and saw my mother bending over me—it was her hand which was so deliciously cool on my brow: I felt amazed somehow. I expected to see her; and yet I was surprised, for I had not seen her for a long time—a long, long time. I knew that she was dead—could I be dead, too? I looked at her again more carefully, and as I looked, the old features died away, but the expression remained the same. And then the dear, well-known face of Mrs Trevor grew slowly before me. She smiled as she saw the look of recognition in my eyes, and, bending down, kissed me very tenderly. As she drew back her head something warm fell on my face. I wondered what this could be, and after thinking for a long time, to do which I closed my eyes, I came to the conclusion that it was a tear. After some more thinking I opened my eyes to see why she was crying; but she was gone, and I could see that although the window-blinds were pulled up the room was almost dark. I felt much more awake and much stronger than I had been before, and tried to call Mrs Trevor. A woman got up from a chair behind the bed-curtains and went to the door, said something, and came back and settled my pillows.

'Where is Mrs Trevor?' I asked, feebly. 'She was here just now.'

The woman smiled at me cheerfully, and answered: 'She will be here in a moment. Dear heart! but she will be glad to see you so strong and sensible.'

After a few minutes she came into the room, and, bending over me, asked me how I felt. I said that I was all right—and then a thought struck me, so I asked, 'What was the matter with me?'

I was told that I had been ill, very ill, but that I was now much better. Something, I know not what, suddenly recalled to my memory all the scene of the bedroom, and the fright which my folly had caused, and I grew quite dizzy with the rush of blood to my head. But Mrs Trevor's arm supported me, and after a time the faintness passed away, and my memory was completely restored. I started violently from the arm that held me up, and called out: 'Is she all right? I heard her say, "saved". Is she all right?'

'Hush, dear boy, hush–she is all right. Do not excite yourself.'

'Are you deceiving me?' I enquired. 'Tell me all–I can bear it. Is she well or no?'

'She has been very ill, but she is now getting strong and well, thank God.'

I began to cry, half from weakness and half from joy, and Mrs Trevor seeing this, and knowing with the sweet instinct of womanhood that I would rather be alone, quickly left the room, after making a sign to the nurse, who sank again to her old place behind the bed-curtain.

I thought for long; and all the time from my first coming to Scarp to the moment of unconsciousness after I sprung through the window came back to me as in a dream. Gradually the room became darker and darker, and my thoughts began to give semblance to the objects around me, till at length the visible world passed away from my wearied eyes, and in my dreams I continued to think of all that had been. I have a hazy recollection of taking some food and then relapsing into sleep; but remember no more distinctly until I woke fully in the morning and found Mrs Trevor again in the room. She came over to my bedside, and sitting down said gaily: 'Ah, Frank, you look bright and strong this morning, dear boy. You will soon be well now I trust.'

Her cool deft fingers settled my pillow and brushed back the hair from my forehead. I took her hand and kissed it, and the doing so made me very happy. By and by I asked her how was Miss Fothering.

'Better, much better this morning. She has been asking after you ever since she has been able; and today when I told her how much better you were she brightened up at once.'

I felt a flush painfully strong rushing over my face as she spoke, but she went on: 'She has asked me to let her see you as soon as both of you are able. She wants to thank you for your conduct on that awful night. But there, I won't tell any more tales–let her tell you what she likes herself.'

'To thank me–me–for what? For having brought her to the verge of madness or perhaps death through my silly fears and imagination. Oh, Mrs Trevor, I know that you never mock anyone–but to me that sounds like mockery.'

She leaned over me as she sat on my bedside and said, oh, so sweetly, yet so firmly that a sense of the truth of her words came at once upon me: 'If I had a son I would wish him to think as you have thought, and to act as you have acted. I would pray for it night and day and if he suffered as you have done, I would lean over him as I lean over you now and feel glad, as I feel now, that he had thought and acted as a true-hearted man should think and act. I would rejoice that God had given me such a son; and if he should die–as I feared at first that you should–I would be a prouder and happier woman kneeling by his dead body than I would in clasping a different son, living, in my arms.'

Oh, how my weak fluttering heart did beat as she spoke. With pity for her blighted maternal instincts, with gladness that a true-hearted woman had approved of my conduct toward a woman whom I loved, and with joy for the deep love for myself. There was no mistaking the honesty of her words–her face was perfectly radiant as she spoke them.

I put up my arms–it took all my strength to do it–round her neck, and whispered softly in her ear one word, 'mother'.

She did not expect it, for it seemed to startle her; but her arms tightened around me convulsively. I could feel a perfect rain of tears falling on my upturned face as I looked into her eyes, full of love and long-sought joy. As I looked I felt stronger and better; my sympathy for her joy did much to restore my strength.

For some little time she was silent, and then she spoke as if to herself, 'God has given me a son at last. I thank thee, O Father; forgive me if I have at any time repined. The son I prayed for might have been different from what I would wish. Thou doest best in all things.'

For some time after this she stayed quite silent, still supporting me in her arms. I felt inexpressibly happy. There was an atmosphere of love around me, for which I had longed all my life. The love of a mother, for which I had pined since my orphan childhood, I had got at last, and the love of a woman to become far dearer to me than a mother I felt was close at hand.

At length I began to feel tired, and Mrs Trevor laid me back on my pillow. It pleased me inexpressibly to observe her kind motherly manner with me now. The ice between us had at last been broken, we had declared our mutual love, and the white-haired woman was as happy in the declaration as the young man.

The next day I felt a shade stronger, and a similar improvement was manifested on the next. Mrs Trevor always attended me herself, and her good reports of Miss Fothering's progress helped to cheer me not a little. And so the days wore on, and many passed away before I was allowed to rise from bed.

One day Mrs Trevor came into the room in a state of suppressed delight. By this time I had been allowed to sit up a little while each day, and was beginning to get strong, or rather less weak, for I was still very helpless.

'Frank, the doctor says that you may be moved into another room tomorrow for a change, and that you may see

Di.'

As may be supposed I was anxious to see Miss Fothering. Whilst I had been able to think during my illness, I had thought about her all day long, and sometimes all night long. I had been in love with her even before that fatal night. My heart told me that secret whilst I was waiting to hear the clock strike, and saw all my folly about the dream; but now I not only loved the woman but I almost worshipped my own bright ideal which was merged in her. The constant series of kind messages that passed between us tended not a little to increase my attachment, and now I eagerly looked forward to a meeting with her face to face.

I awoke earlier than usual next morning, and grew rather feverish as the time for our interview approached. However, I soon cooled down upon a vague threat being held out, that if I did not become more composed I must defer my visit.

The expected time at length arrived, and I was wheeled in my chair into Mrs Trevor's boudoir. As I entered the door I looked eagerly round and saw, seated in another chair near one of the windows, a girl, who, turning her head round languidly, disclosed the features of Miss Fothering. She was very pale and ethereal looking, and seemed extremely delicate; but in my opinion this only heightened her natural beauty. As she caught sight of me a beautiful blush rushed over her poor, pale face, and even tinged her alabaster forehead. This passed quickly, and she became calm again, and paler than before. My chair was wheeled over to her, and Mrs Trevor said, as she bent over and kissed her, after soothing the pillow in her chair: 'Di, my love, I have brought Frank to see you. You may talk together for a little while; but, mind, the doctor's orders are very strict, and if either of you excite yourselves about anything I must forbid you to meet again until you are both much stronger.'

She said the last words as she was leaving the room.

I felt red and pale, hot and cold by turns. I looked at Miss Fothering and faltered. However, in a moment or two I summoned up courage to address her.

'Miss Fothering, I hope you forgive me for the pain and danger I caused you by that foolish fear of mine. I assure you that nothing I ever did—'

Here she interrupted me. 'Mr Stanford, I beg you will not talk like that. I must thank you for the care you thought me worthy of. I will not say how proud I feel of it, and for the generous courage and wisdom you displayed in rescuing me from the terror of that awful scene.'

She grew pale, even paler than she had been before, as she spoke the last words, and trembled all over. I feared for her, and said as cheerfully as I could: 'Don't be alarmed. Do calm yourself. That is all over now and past. Don't let its horror disturb you ever again.'

My speaking, although it calmed her somewhat, was not sufficient to banish her fear, and, seeing that she was really excited, I called to Mrs Trevor, who came in from the next room and talked to us for a little while. She gradually did away with Miss Fothering's fear by her pleasant cheery conversation. She, poor girl, had received a sad shock, and the thought that I had been the cause of it gave me great anguish. After a little quiet chat, however, I grew more cheerful, but presently feeling faintish, was wheeled back to my own room and put to bed.

For many long days I continued very weak, and hardly made any advance. I saw Miss Fothering every day, and each day I loved her more and more. She got stronger as the days advanced, and after a few weeks was comparatively in good health, but still I continued weak. Her illness had been merely the result of the fright she had sustained on that unhappy night; but mine was the nervous prostration consequent on the long period of anxiety between the dream and its seeming fulfilment, united with the physical weakness resulting from my wounds caused by jumping through the window. During all this time of weakness Mrs Trevor was, indeed, a mother to me. She watched me day and night, and as far as a woman could, made my life a dream of happiness. But the crowning glory of that time was the thought that sometimes forced itself upon me—that Diana cared for me.

She continued to remain at Scarp by Mrs Trevor's request, as her father had gone to the Continent for the winter, and with my adopted mother she shared the attendance on me. Day after day her care for my every want grew greater, till I came to fancy her like a guardian angel keeping watch over me. With the peculiar delicate sense that accompanies extreme physical prostration I could see that the growth of her pity kept pace with the growth of her strength. My love kept pace with both. I often wondered if it could be sympathy and not pity that so forestalled my wants and wishes; or if it could be love that answered in her heart when mine beat for her. She only showed pity and tenderness in her acts and words, but still I hoped and longed for something more.

Those days of my long-continued weakness were to me sweet, sweet days. I used to watch her for hours as she sat opposite to me reading or working, and my eyes would fill with tears as I thought how hard it would be to die and leave her behind me. So strong was the flame of my love that I believed, in spite of my religious teaching, that, should I die, I would leave the better part of my being behind me. I used to think in a vague imaginative way, that was no less powerful because it was undefined, of what speeches I would make to her—if I were well. How I would talk to her in nobler language than that in which I would now allow my thoughts to mould themselves. How, as I talked, my passion, and honesty, and purity would make me so eloquent that she would love to hear me speak. How I would wander with her through the sunny gladed woods that stretched away before me through the open window, and sit by her feet on a mossy bank beside some purling brook that rippled gaily over the stones, gazing into the depths of her eyes, where my future life was pictured in one long sheen of light. How I would whisper in her ear sweet words that would make me tremble to speak them, and her tremble to hear. How she would bend to me and show me her love by letting me tell her mine without reproof. And then would come, like the shadow of a sudden rain–cloud over an April landscape, the bitter, bitter thought that all this longing was but a dream, and that when the time had come when such things might have been, I would, most likely, be sleeping under the green turf. And she might, perhaps, be weeping in the silence of her chamber sad, sad tears for her blighted love and for me.

Then my thoughts would become less selfish, and I would try to imagine the bitter blow of my death–if she loved me–for I knew that a woman loves not-by the value of what she loves, but by the strength of her affection and admiration for her own ideal, which she thinks she sees bodied forth in some man. But these thoughts had always the proviso that the dreams of happiness were prophetic. Alas! I had altogether lost faith in dreams. Still, I could not but feel that even if I had never frightened Miss Fothering by telling my vision, she might, nevertheless, have been terrified by the effect of the moonlight upon the flowers of the pampas tufts, and that, under Providence, I was the instrument of saving her from a shock even greater than that which she did experience, for help might not have come to her so soon. This thought always gave me hope. Whenever I thought of her sorrow for my death, I would find my eyes filled with a sudden rush of tears which would shut out from my waking vision the object of my thoughts and fears. Then she would come over to me and place her cool hand on my forehead, and whisper sweet words of comfort and hope in my ears. As I would feel her warm breath upon my cheek and wafting my hair from my brow, I would lose all sense of pain and sorrow and care, and live only in the brightness of the present. At such times I would cry silently from very happiness, for I was sadly weak, and even trifling things touched me deeply. Many a stray memory of some tender word heard or some gentle deed done, or of some sorrow or distress, would set me thinking for hours and stir all the tender feelings of my nature.

Slowly–very slowly–I began to get stronger, but for many days more I was almost completely helpless. With returning strength came the strengthening of my passion–for passion my love for Diana had become. She had been so woven into my thoughts that my love for her was a part of my being, and I felt that away from her my future life would be but a bare existence and no more. But strange to say, with increasing strength and passion came increasing diffidence. I felt in her presence so bashful and timorous that I hardly dared to look at her, and could not speak save to answer an occasional question. I had ceased to dream entirely, for such daydreams as I used to have seemed now wild and almost sacrilegious to my overexcited imagination. But when she was not looking at me I would be happy in merely seeing her or hearing her speak. I could tell the moment she left the house or entered it, and her footfall was the music sweetest to my ears—except her voice. Sometimes she would catch sight of my bashful looks at her, and then, at my conscious blushing, a bright smile would flit over her face. It was sweet and womanly, but sometimes I would think that it was no more than her pity finding expression. She was always in my thoughts and these doubts and fears constantly assailed me, so that I could feel that the brooding over the subject—a matter which I was powerless to prevent—was doing me an injury; perhaps seriously retarding my recovery.

One day I felt very sad. There had a bitter sense of loneliness come over me which was unusual. It was a good sign of returning health, for it was like the waking from a dream to a world of fact, with all its troubles and cares. There was a sense of coldness and loneliness in the world, and I felt that I had lost something without gaining anything in return–I had, in fact, lost somewhat of my sense of dependence, which is a consequence of prostration, but had not yet regained my strength. I sat opposite a window itself in shade, but looking over a garden that in the summer had been bright with flowers, and sweet with their odours, but which, now, was lit up only in patches by the quiet mellow gleams of the autumn sun, and brightened by a few stray flowers that had survived the first frosts.

As I sat I could not help thinking of what my future would be. I felt that I was getting strong, and the possibilities of my life seemed very real to me. How I longed for courage to ask Diana to be my wife! Any certainty would be better than the suspense I now constantly endured. I had but little hope that she would accept me, for she seemed to care less for me now than in the early days of my illness. As I grew stronger she seemed to hold somewhat aloof from me; and as my fears and doubts grew more and more, I could hardly bear to think of my joy should she accept me, or of my despair should she refuse. Either emotion seemed too great to be borne.

Today when she entered the room my fears were vastly increased. She seemed much stronger than usual, for a glow, as of health, ruddied her cheeks, and she seemed so lovely that I could not conceive that such a woman would ever condescend to be my wife. There was an unusual constraint in her manner as she came and spoke to me, and flitted round me, doing in her own graceful way all the thousand little offices that only a woman's hand can do for an invalid. She turned to me two or three times, as if she was about to speak; but turned away again, each time silent, and with a blush. I could see that her heart was beating violently. At length she spoke.

'Frank.'

Oh! what a wild throb went through me as I heard my name from her lips for the first time. The blood rushed to my head, so that for a moment I was quite faint. Her cool hand on my forehead revived me.

'Frank, will you let me speak to you for a few minutes as honestly as I would wish to speak, and as freely?'

'Go on.'

'You will promise me not to think me unwomanly or forward, for indeed I act from the best motives–promise me?'

This was said slowly with much hesitation, and a convulsive heaving of the chest.

'I promise.'

'We can see that you are not getting as strong as you ought, and the doctor says that there is some idea too much in your mind—that you brood over it, and that it is retarding your recovery. Mrs Trevor and I have been talking about it. We have been comparing notes, and I think we have found out what your idea is. Now, Frank, you must not pale and red like that, or I will have to leave off.'

'I will be calm—indeed, I will. Go on.'

'We both thought that it might do you good to talk to you freely, and we want to know if our idea is correct. Mrs Trevor thought it better that I should speak to you than she should.'

'What is the idea?'

Hitherto, although she had manifested considerable emotion, her voice had been full and clear, but she answered this last question very faintly, and with much hesitation.

'You are attached to me, and you are afraid I—I don't love you.'

Here her voice was checked by a rush of tears, and she turned her head away.

'Diana,' said I, 'dear Diana,' and I held out my arms with what strength I had.

The colour rushed over her face and neck, and then she turned, and with a convulsive sigh laid her head upon my shoulder. One weak arm fell round her waist, and my other hand rested on her head. I said nothing. I could not speak, but I felt the beating of her heart against mine, and thought that if I died then I must be happy for ever, if there be memory in the other world.

For a long, long, blissful time she kept her place, and gradually our hearts ceased to beat so violently, and we became calm.

Such was the confession of our love. No plighted faith, no passionate vows, but the silence and the thrill of sympathy through our hearts were sweeter than words could be.

Diana raised her head and looked fearlessly but appealingly into my eyes as she asked me: 'Oh, Frank, did I do right to speak? Could it have been better if I had waited?'

She saw my wishes in my eyes, and bent down her head to me. I kissed her on the forehead and fervently prayed, 'Thank God that all was as it has been. May He bless my own darling wife for ever and ever.'

'Amen,' said a sweet, tender voice.

We both looked up without shame, for we knew the tones of my second mother. Her face, streaming with tears of joy, was lit up by a sudden ray of sunlight through the casement.